STAR WARS®

THE CLONE WARS™

HERO OF THE CONFEDERACY
VOLUME ONE

BREAKING BREAD WITH THE ENEMY!

SCRIPT
HENRY GILROY
STEVEN MELCHING

PENCILS
BRIAN KOSCHAK

INKS
DAN PARSONS

COLORS
MICHAEL E. WIGGAM

LETTERING
MICHAEL HEISLER

COVER ART
RAMÓN PÉREZ

Nonaligned worlds continue to trade with the Separatists. Some Senators demand that these worlds sign an oath of loyalty to the Republic, while others defend their right to remain neutral. The debate may force some of the wealthiest planets in the galaxy to join the Confederacy of Independent Systems.

Meanwhile, the Republic launches a broad counterattack after a string of Separatist victories. Under the command of Jedi Generals Anakin Skywalker, Obi-Wan Kenobi, and Mace Windu, the clone army has recaptured a key hyperspace supply route and liberated dozens of worlds from the oppressive grip of Count Dooku.

But the Separatists are far from defeated. They strike back with a powerful new class of droid fighters that gives them a clear advantage in the battle for space superiority . . .

DARK HORSE COMICS

Visit us at www.abdopublishing.com

Reinforced library bound edition published in 2011 by Spotlight, a division of the ABDO Group, 8000 West 78th Street, Edina, Minnesota 55439. Spotlight produces high-quality reinforced library bound editions for schools and libraries. Published by agreement with Dark Horse Comics, Inc., and Lucasfilm Ltd.

Printed in the United States of America, North Mankato, Minnesota.
102010
012011
This book contains at least 10% recycled materials.

Cataloging-in-Publication Data

Gilroy, Henry.
 Hero of the Confederacy Vol. 1: breaking bread with the enemy! / story, Henry Gilroy and Steve Melching ; art, Brian Koschak. --Reinforced library bound ed.
    v. cm. -- (Star wars: the clone wars)
    "Dark Horse Comics."
 ISBN 978-1-59961-841-8 (v. 1)
 1. Graphic novels. [1. Graphic novels.] I. Melching, Steve. II. Koschak, Brian, ill. III. Star Wars, the clone wars (television program) IV. Title.
 PZ7.7.G55He 2011.
 741.5'973

All Spotlight books have reinforced library bindings and are manufactured in the United States of America.

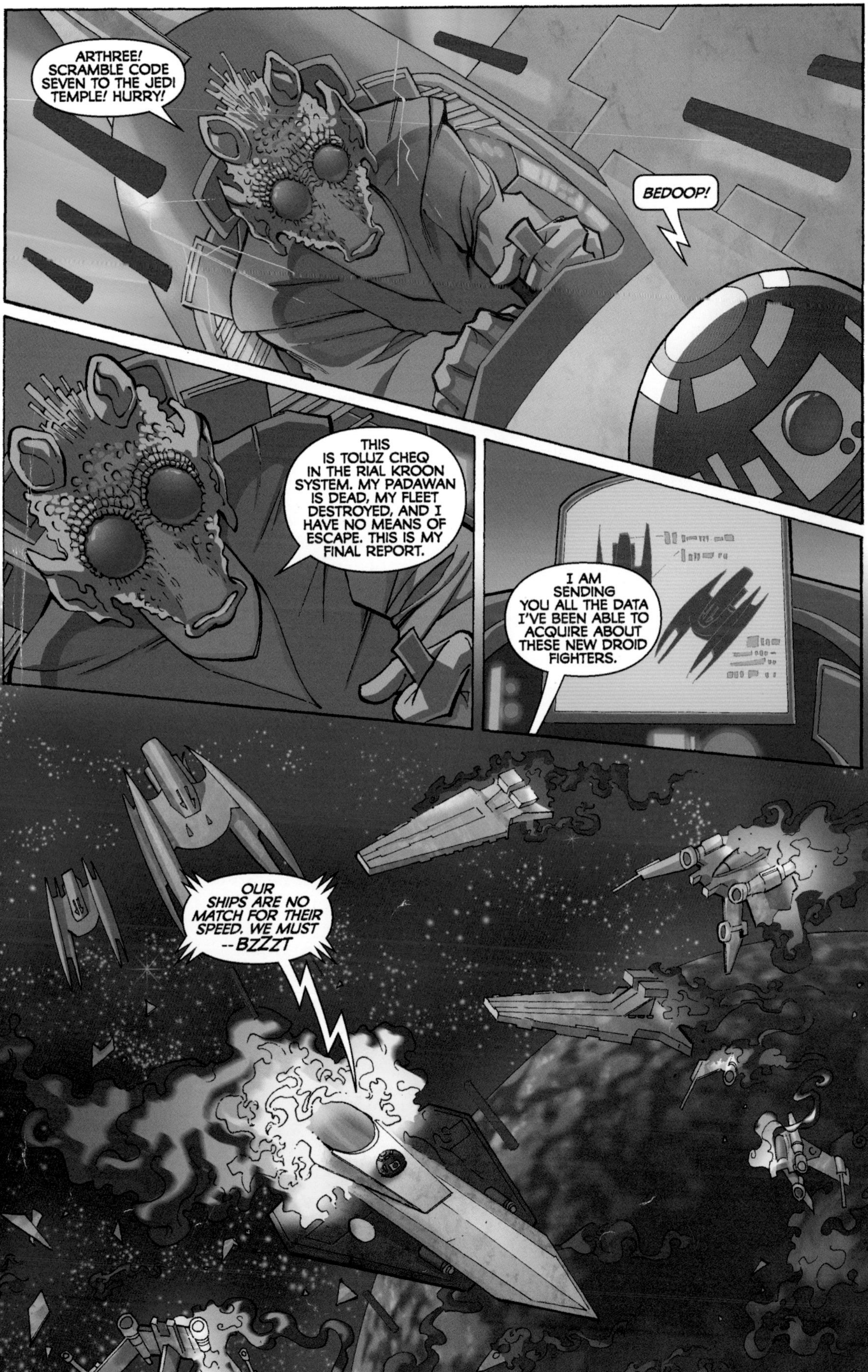
ARTHREE! SCRAMBLE CODE SEVEN TO THE JEDI TEMPLE! HURRY!
BEDOOP!
THIS IS TOLUZ CHEQ IN THE RIAL KROON SYSTEM. MY PADAWAN IS DEAD, MY FLEET DESTROYED, AND I HAVE NO MEANS OF ESCAPE. THIS IS MY FINAL REPORT.
I AM SENDING YOU ALL THE DATA I'VE BEEN ABLE TO ACQUIRE ABOUT THESE NEW DROID FIGHTERS.
OUR SHIPS ARE NO MATCH FOR THEIR SPEED. WE MUST --BZZZT

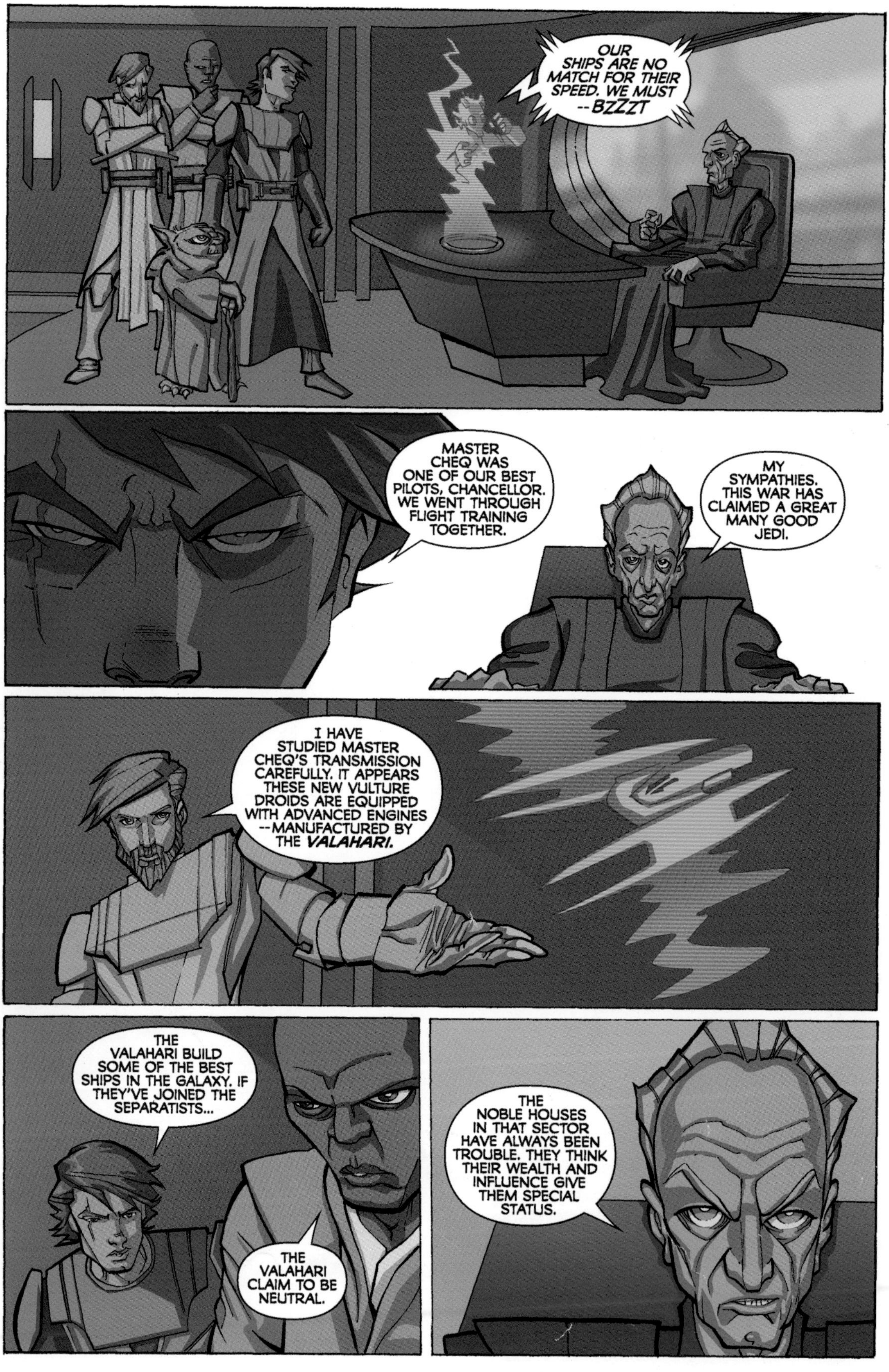
OUR SHIPS ARE NO MATCH FOR THEIR SPEED. WE MUST --BZZZT
MASTER CHEQ WAS ONE OF OUR BEST PILOTS, CHANCELLOR. WE WENT THROUGH FLIGHT TRAINING TOGETHER.
MY SYMPATHIES. THIS WAR HAS CLAIMED A GREAT MANY GOOD JEDI.
I HAVE STUDIED MASTER CHEQ'S TRANSMISSION CAREFULLY. IT APPEARS THESE NEW VULTURE DROIDS ARE EQUIPPED WITH ADVANCED ENGINES --MANUFACTURED BY THE VALAHARI.
THE VALAHARI BUILD SOME OF THE BEST SHIPS IN THE GALAXY. IF THEY'VE JOINED THE SEPARATISTS...
THE VALAHARI CLAIM TO BE NEUTRAL.
THE NOBLE HOUSES IN THAT SECTOR HAVE ALWAYS BEEN TROUBLE. THEY THINK THEIR WEALTH AND INFLUENCE GIVE THEM SPECIAL STATUS.

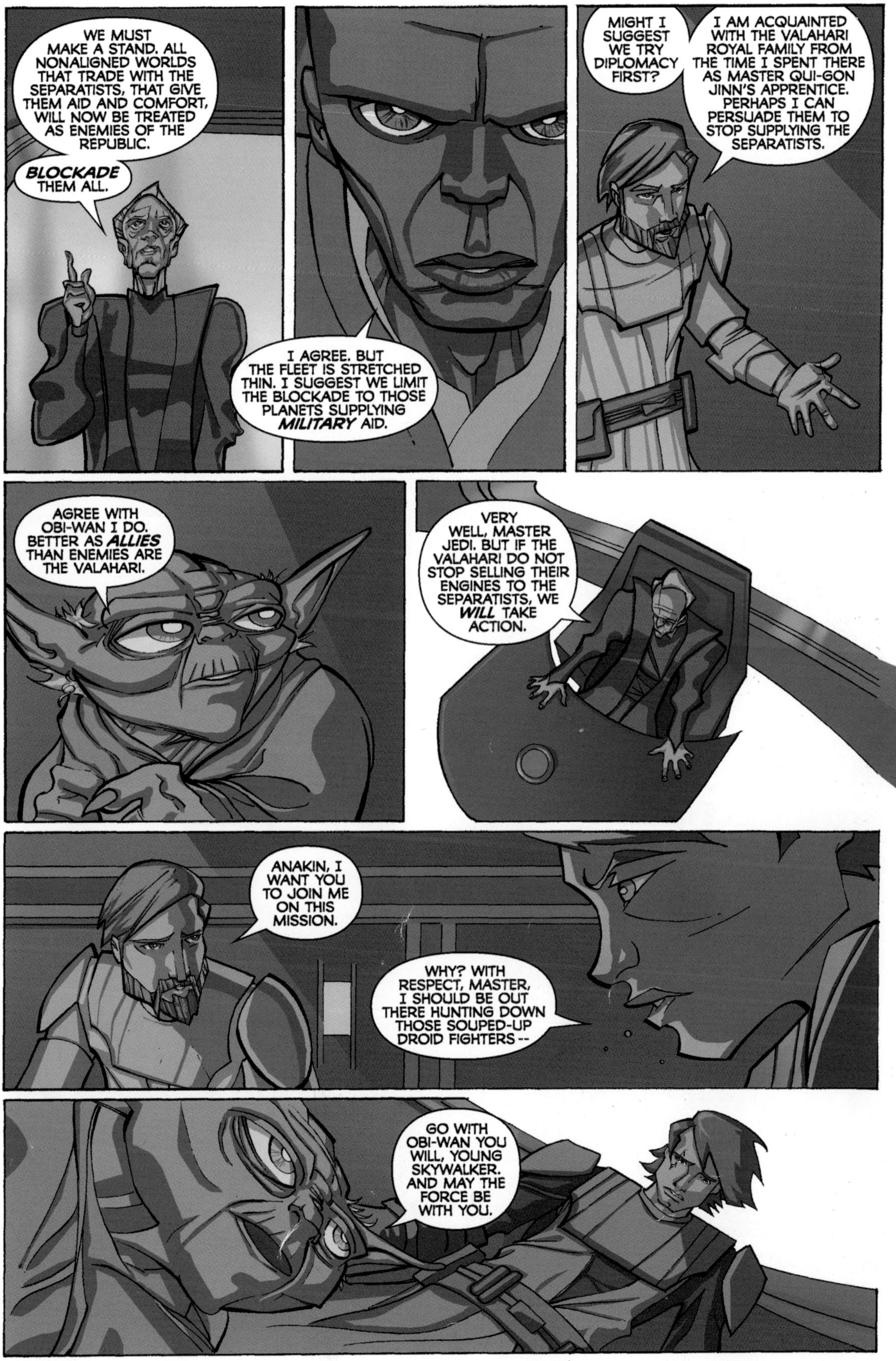

WE MUST MAKE A STAND. ALL NONALIGNED WORLDS THAT TRADE WITH THE SEPARATISTS, THAT GIVE THEM AID AND COMFORT, WILL NOW BE TREATED AS ENEMIES OF THE REPUBLIC.
BLOCKADE THEM ALL.
I AGREE. BUT THE FLEET IS STRETCHED THIN. I SUGGEST WE LIMIT THE BLOCKADE TO THOSE PLANETS SUPPLYING *MILITARY* AID.
MIGHT I SUGGEST WE TRY DIPLOMACY FIRST?
I AM ACQUAINTED WITH THE VALAHARI ROYAL FAMILY FROM THE TIME I SPENT THERE AS MASTER QUI-GON JINN'S APPRENTICE. PERHAPS I CAN PERSUADE THEM TO STOP SUPPLYING THE SEPARATISTS.
AGREE WITH OBI-WAN I DO. BETTER AS *ALLIES* THAN ENEMIES ARE THE VALAHARI.
VERY WELL, MASTER JEDI. BUT IF THE VALAHARI DO NOT STOP SELLING THEIR ENGINES TO THE SEPARATISTS, WE *WILL* TAKE ACTION.
ANAKIN, I WANT YOU TO JOIN ME ON THIS MISSION.
WHY? WITH RESPECT, MASTER, I SHOULD BE OUT THERE HUNTING DOWN THOSE SOUPED-UP DROID FIGHTERS --
GO WITH OBI-WAN YOU WILL, YOUNG SKYWALKER. AND MAY THE FORCE BE WITH YOU.

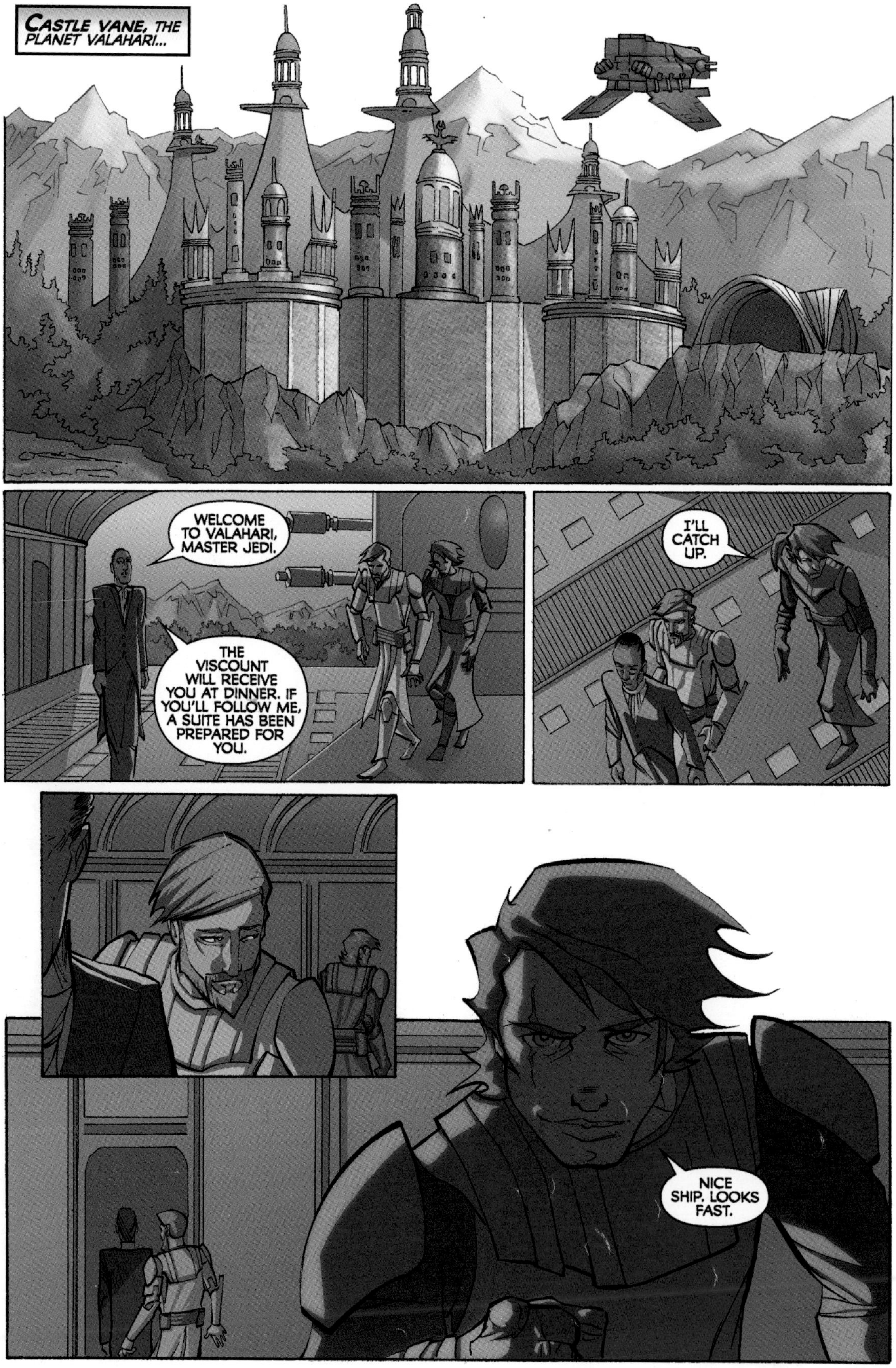
CASTLE VANE, THE PLANET VALAHARI...
WELCOME TO VALAHARI, MASTER JEDI.
THE VISCOUNT WILL RECEIVE YOU AT DINNER. IF YOU'LL FOLLOW ME, A SUITE HAS BEEN PREPARED FOR YOU.
I'LL CATCH UP.
NICE SHIP. LOOKS FAST.

FASTEST SHIP IN THE SECTOR.

THINK SO?

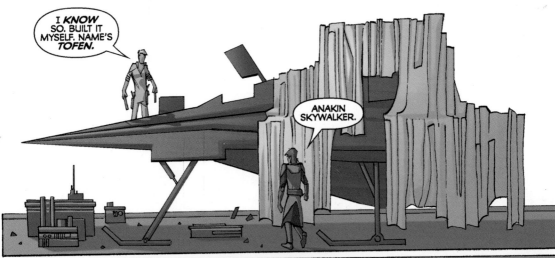

I *KNOW* SO. BUILT IT MYSELF. NAME'S *TOFEN*.

ANAKIN SKYWALKER.

SKYWALKER? THE GREAT HERO OF THE REPUBLIC? WITH ONE THOUSAND NINE HUNDRED AND EIGHTY STARFIGHTER KILLS?

I HAVEN'T BEEN KEEPING COUNT.

SOME SAY YOU'RE THE BEST STARPILOT IN THE GALAXY. YOU KNOW... I'VE GOT A COUPLE OF PODRACERS WE CAN TAKE OUT.

UNLESS YOU'RE AFRAID YOU MIGHT LOSE.

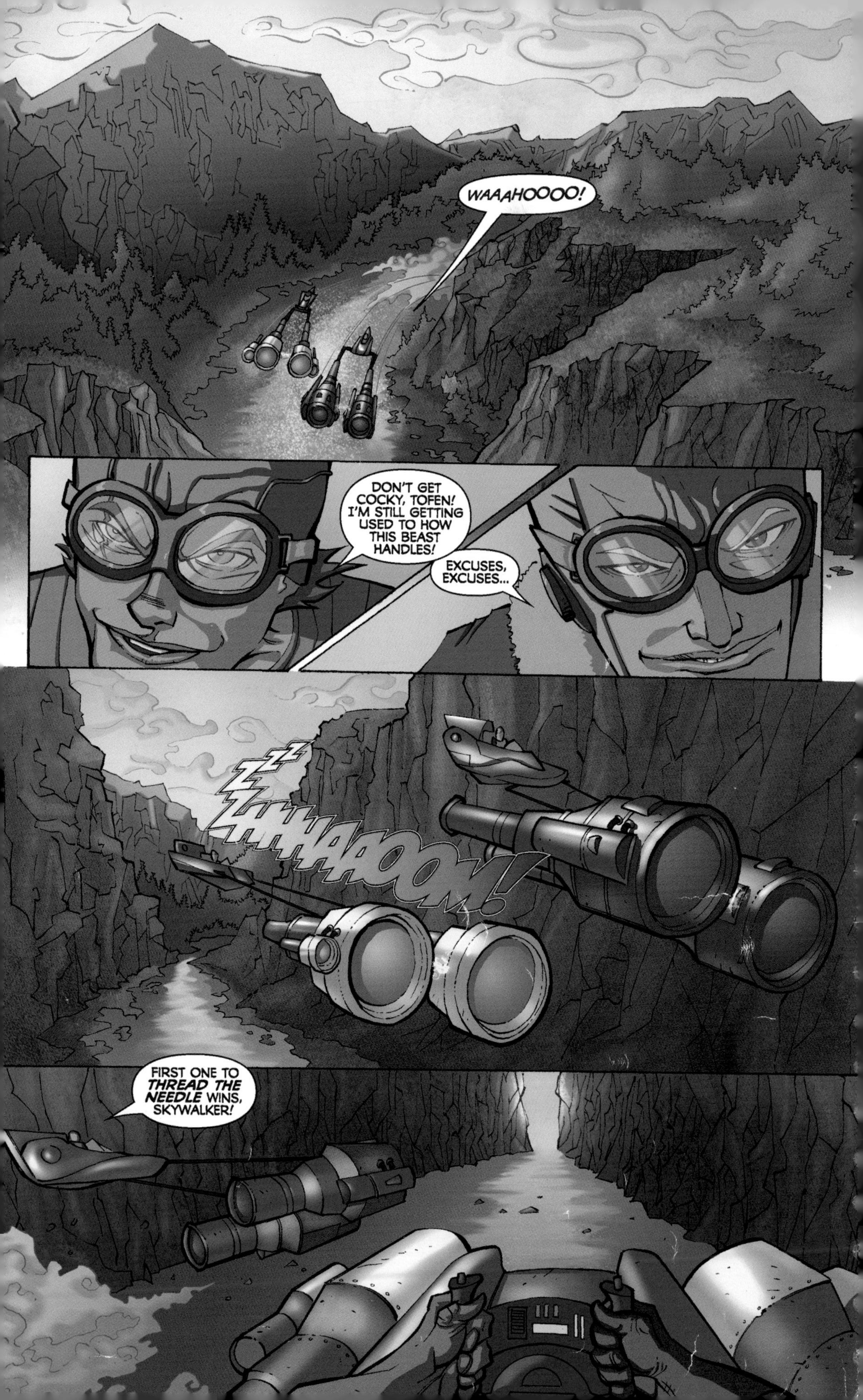
WAAAHOOOO!
DON'T GET COCKY, TOFEN! I'M STILL GETTING USED TO HOW THIS BEAST HANDLES!
EXCUSES, EXCUSES...
ZZZ ZHHHAAOOM!
FIRST ONE TO THREAD THE NEEDLE WINS, SKYWALKER!

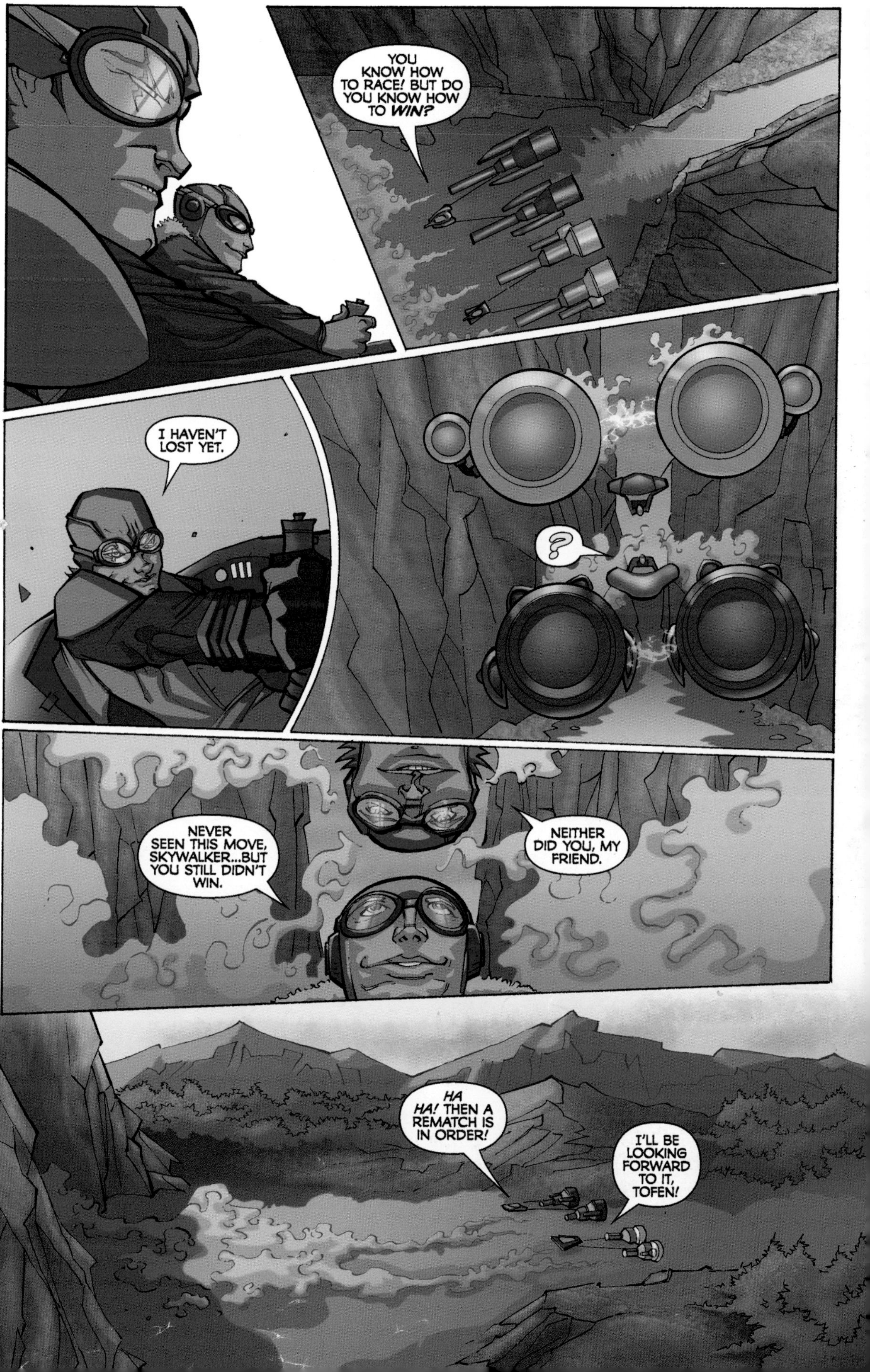
YOU KNOW HOW TO RACE! BUT DO YOU KNOW HOW TO *WIN?*
I HAVEN'T LOST YET.
?
NEVER SEEN THIS MOVE, SKYWALKER...BUT YOU STILL DIDN'T WIN.
NEITHER DID YOU, MY FRIEND.
HA HA! THEN A REMATCH IS IN ORDER!
I'LL BE LOOKING FORWARD TO IT, TOFEN!

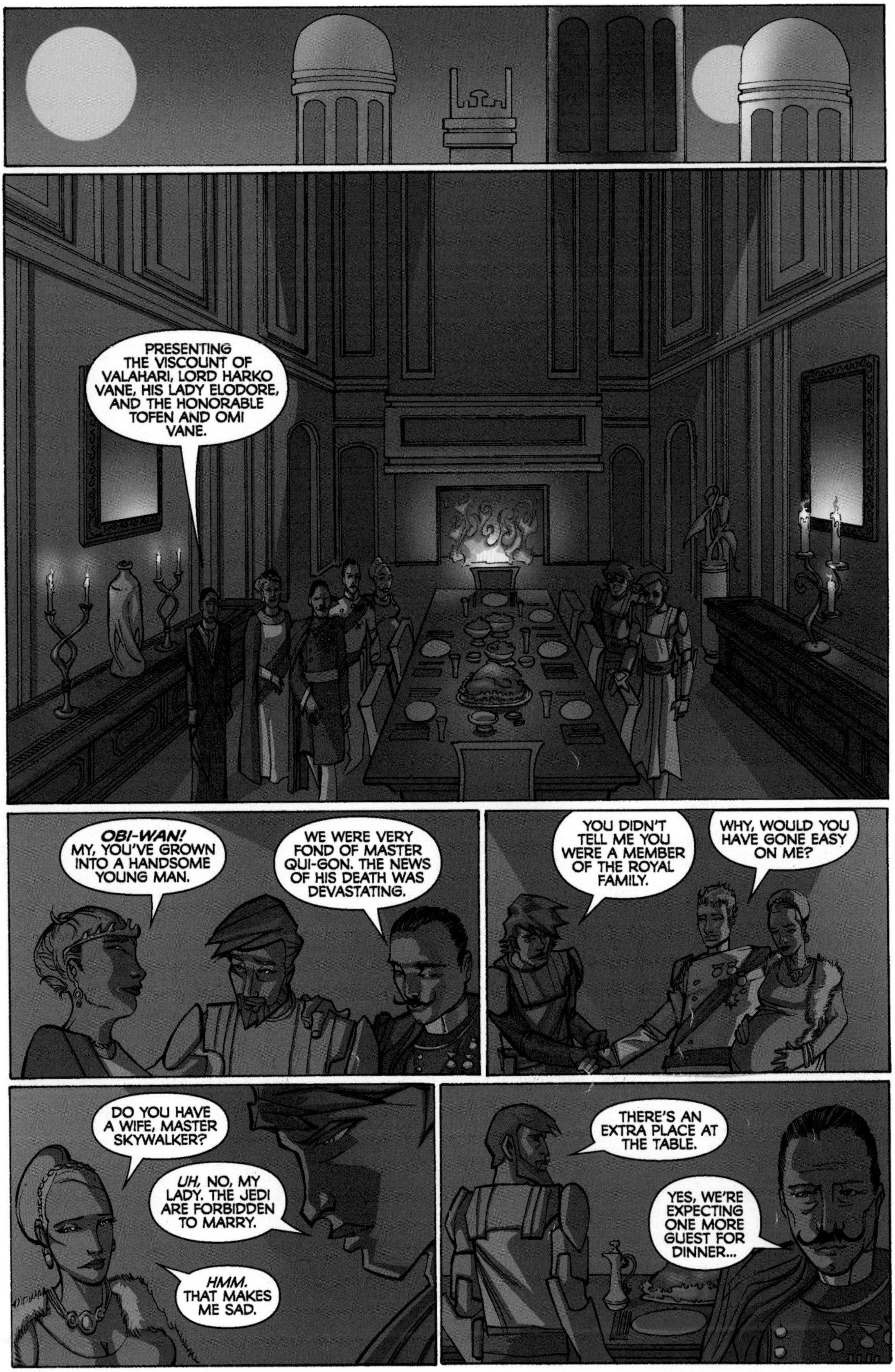
PRESENTING THE VISCOUNT OF VALAHARI, LORD HARKO VANE, HIS LADY ELODORE, AND THE HONORABLE TOFEN AND OMI VANE.
OBI-WAN! MY, YOU'VE GROWN INTO A HANDSOME YOUNG MAN.
WE WERE VERY FOND OF MASTER QUI-GON. THE NEWS OF HIS DEATH WAS DEVASTATING.
YOU DIDN'T TELL ME YOU WERE A MEMBER OF THE ROYAL FAMILY.
WHY, WOULD YOU HAVE GONE EASY ON ME?
DO YOU HAVE A WIFE, MASTER SKYWALKER?
UH, NO, MY LADY. THE JEDI ARE FORBIDDEN TO MARRY.
HMM. THAT MAKES ME SAD.
THERE'S AN EXTRA PLACE AT THE TABLE.
YES, WE'RE EXPECTING ONE MORE GUEST FOR DINNER...

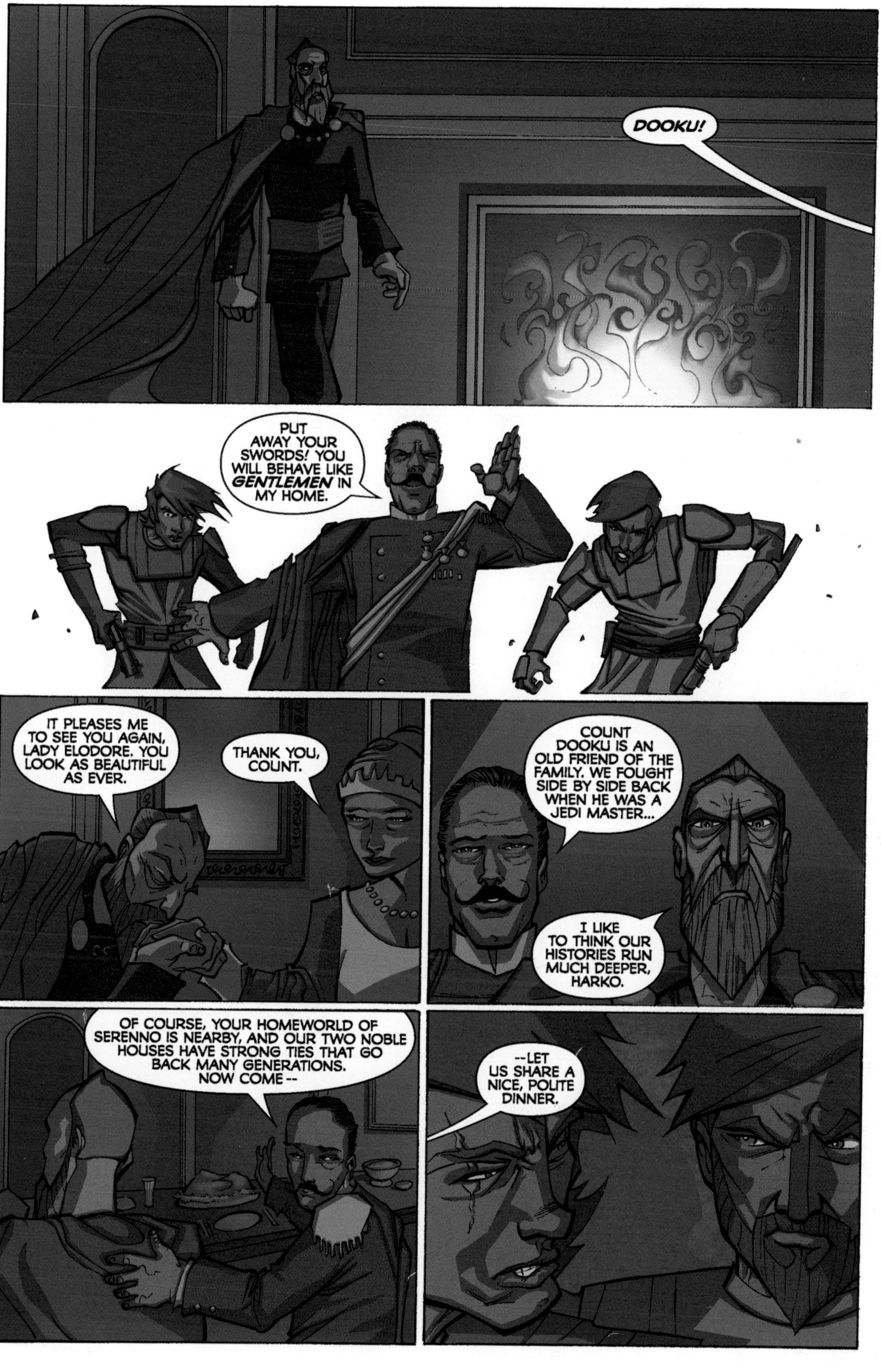
DOOKU!
PUT AWAY YOUR SWORDS! YOU WILL BEHAVE LIKE GENTLEMEN IN MY HOME.
IT PLEASES ME TO SEE YOU AGAIN, LADY ELODORE. YOU LOOK AS BEAUTIFUL AS EVER.
THANK YOU, COUNT.
COUNT DOOKU IS AN OLD FRIEND OF THE FAMILY. WE FOUGHT SIDE BY SIDE BACK WHEN HE WAS A JEDI MASTER...
I LIKE TO THINK OUR HISTORIES RUN MUCH DEEPER, HARKO.
OF COURSE, YOUR HOMEWORLD OF SERENNO IS NEARBY, AND OUR TWO NOBLE HOUSES HAVE STRONG TIES THAT GO BACK MANY GENERATIONS. NOW COME--
--LET US SHARE A NICE, POLITE DINNER.

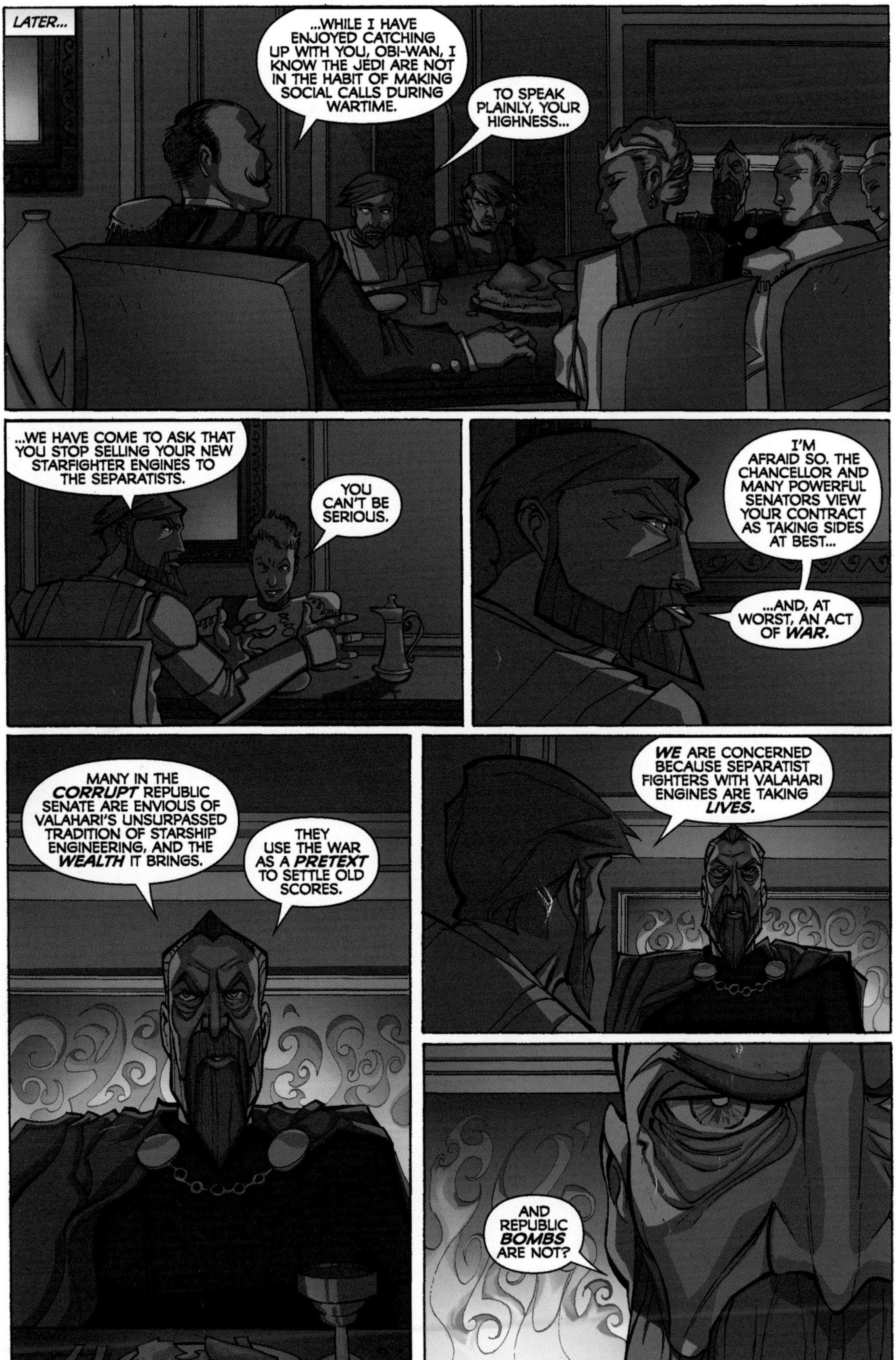
LATER...
...WHILE I HAVE ENJOYED CATCHING UP WITH YOU, OBI-WAN, I KNOW THE JEDI ARE NOT IN THE HABIT OF MAKING SOCIAL CALLS DURING WARTIME.
TO SPEAK PLAINLY, YOUR HIGHNESS...
...WE HAVE COME TO ASK THAT YOU STOP SELLING YOUR NEW STARFIGHTER ENGINES TO THE SEPARATISTS.
YOU CAN'T BE SERIOUS.
I'M AFRAID SO. THE CHANCELLOR AND MANY POWERFUL SENATORS VIEW YOUR CONTRACT AS TAKING SIDES AT BEST...
...AND, AT WORST, AN ACT OF WAR.
MANY IN THE CORRUPT REPUBLIC SENATE ARE ENVIOUS OF VALAHARI'S UNSURPASSED TRADITION OF STARSHIP ENGINEERING, AND THE WEALTH IT BRINGS.
THEY USE THE WAR AS A PRETEXT TO SETTLE OLD SCORES.
WE ARE CONCERNED BECAUSE SEPARATIST FIGHTERS WITH VALAHARI ENGINES ARE TAKING LIVES.
AND REPUBLIC BOMBS ARE NOT?

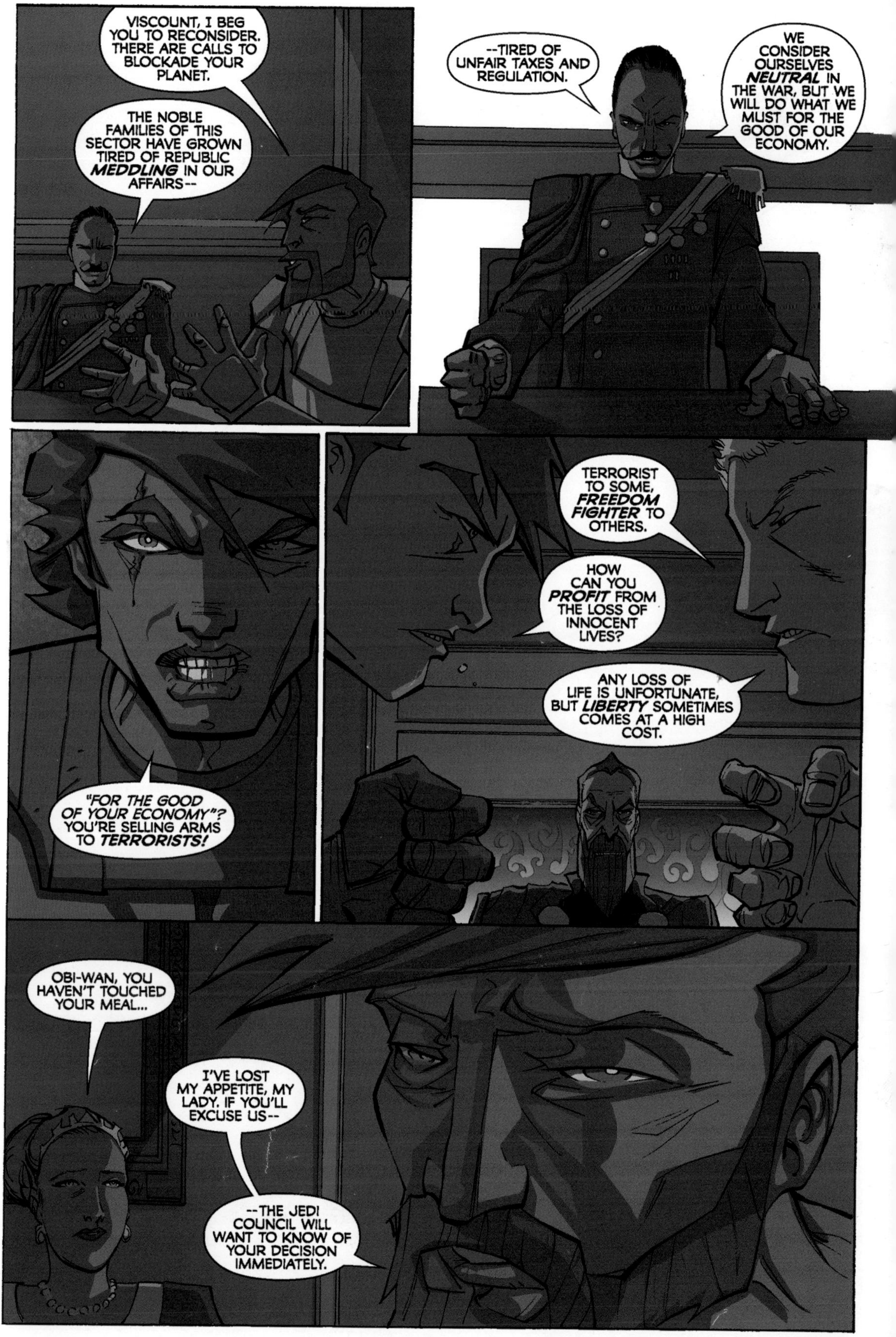
VISCOUNT, I BEG YOU TO RECONSIDER. THERE ARE CALLS TO BLOCKADE YOUR PLANET.
THE NOBLE FAMILIES OF THIS SECTOR HAVE GROWN TIRED OF REPUBLIC MEDDLING IN OUR AFFAIRS--
--TIRED OF UNFAIR TAXES AND REGULATION.
WE CONSIDER OURSELVES NEUTRAL IN THE WAR, BUT WE WILL DO WHAT WE MUST FOR THE GOOD OF OUR ECONOMY.
"FOR THE GOOD OF YOUR ECONOMY"? YOU'RE SELLING ARMS TO TERRORISTS!
TERRORIST TO SOME, FREEDOM FIGHTER TO OTHERS.
HOW CAN YOU PROFIT FROM THE LOSS OF INNOCENT LIVES?
ANY LOSS OF LIFE IS UNFORTUNATE, BUT LIBERTY SOMETIMES COMES AT A HIGH COST.
OBI-WAN, YOU HAVEN'T TOUCHED YOUR MEAL...
I'VE LOST MY APPETITE, MY LADY. IF YOU'LL EXCUSE US--
--THE JEDI COUNCIL WILL WANT TO KNOW OF YOUR DECISION IMMEDIATELY.

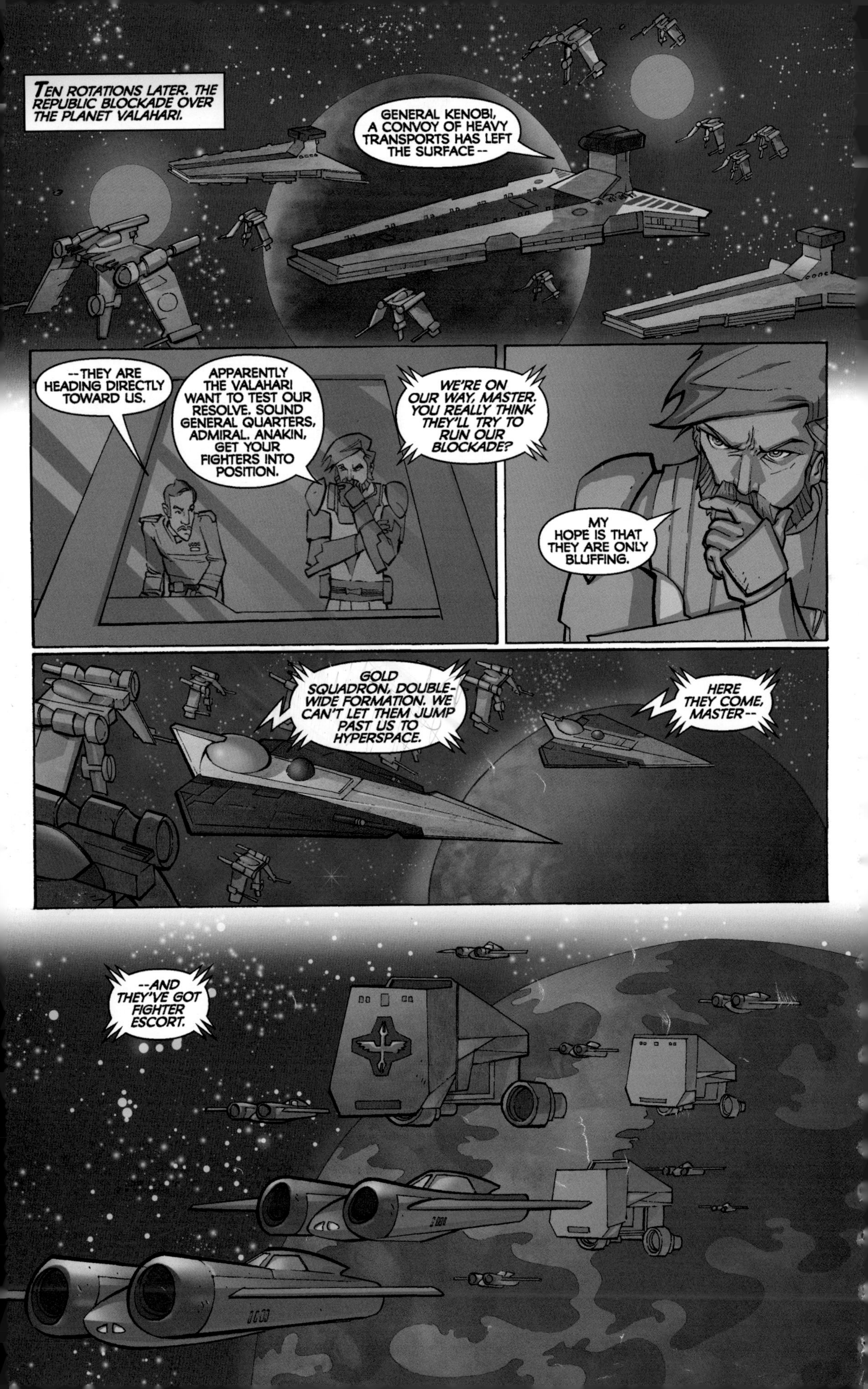
TEN ROTATIONS LATER. THE REPUBLIC BLOCKADE OVER THE PLANET VALAHARI.
GENERAL KENOBI, A CONVOY OF HEAVY TRANSPORTS HAS LEFT THE SURFACE --
--THEY ARE HEADING DIRECTLY TOWARD US.
APPARENTLY THE VALAHARI WANT TO TEST OUR RESOLVE. SOUND GENERAL QUARTERS, ADMIRAL. ANAKIN, GET YOUR FIGHTERS INTO POSITION.
WE'RE ON OUR WAY, MASTER. YOU REALLY THINK THEY'LL TRY TO RUN OUR BLOCKADE?
MY HOPE IS THAT THEY ARE ONLY BLUFFING.
GOLD SQUADRON, DOUBLE-WIDE FORMATION. WE CAN'T LET THEM JUMP PAST US TO HYPERSPACE.
HERE THEY COME, MASTER--
--AND THEY'VE GOT FIGHTER ESCORT.

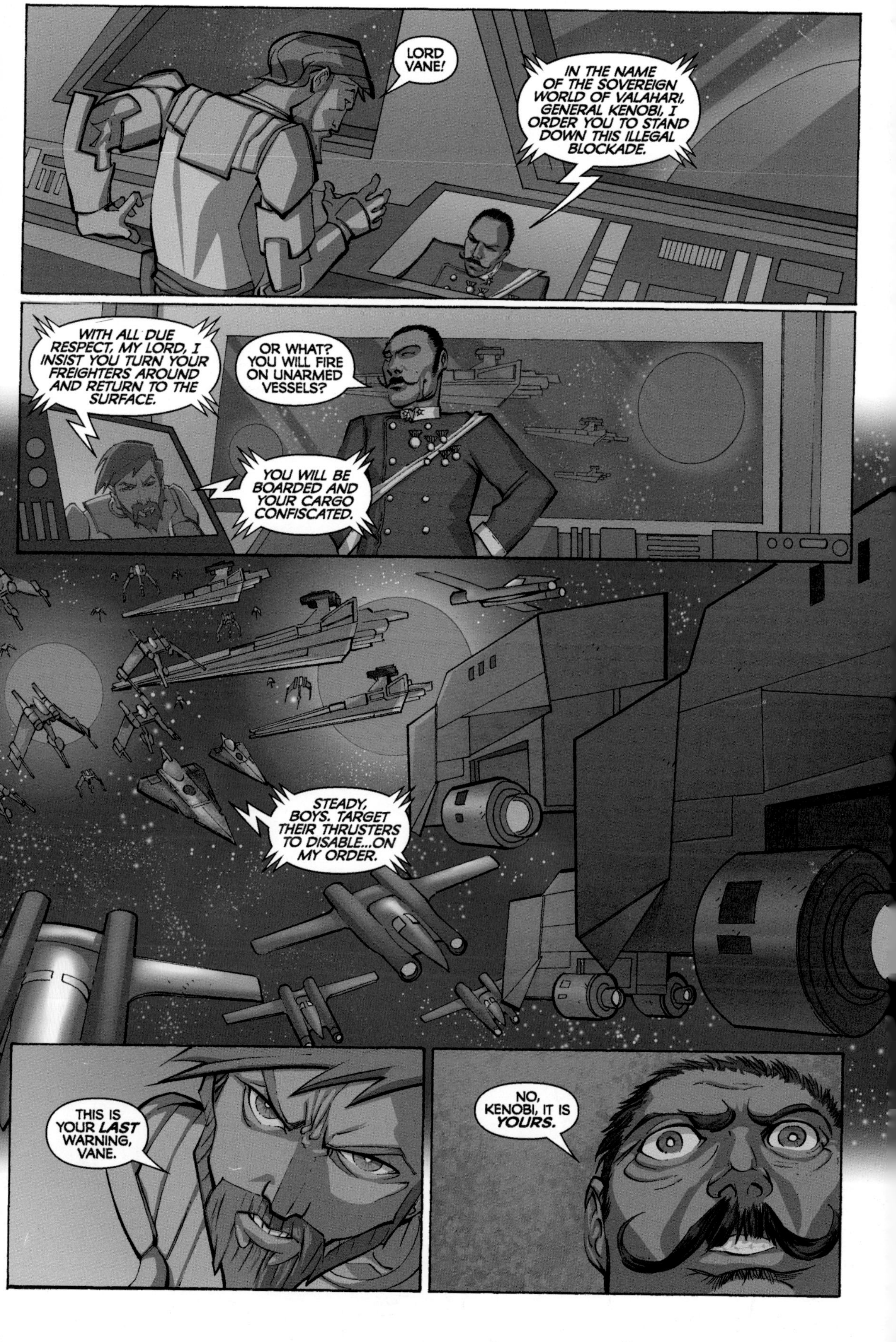
LORD VANE!
IN THE NAME OF THE SOVEREIGN WORLD OF VALAHARI, GENERAL KENOBI, I ORDER YOU TO STAND DOWN THIS ILLEGAL BLOCKADE.
WITH ALL DUE RESPECT, MY LORD, I INSIST YOU TURN YOUR FREIGHTERS AROUND AND RETURN TO THE SURFACE.
OR WHAT? YOU WILL FIRE ON UNARMED VESSELS?
YOU WILL BE BOARDED AND YOUR CARGO CONFISCATED.
STEADY, BOYS. TARGET THEIR THRUSTERS TO DISABLE...ON MY ORDER.
THIS IS YOUR *LAST* WARNING, VANE.
NO, KENOBI, IT IS *YOURS*.

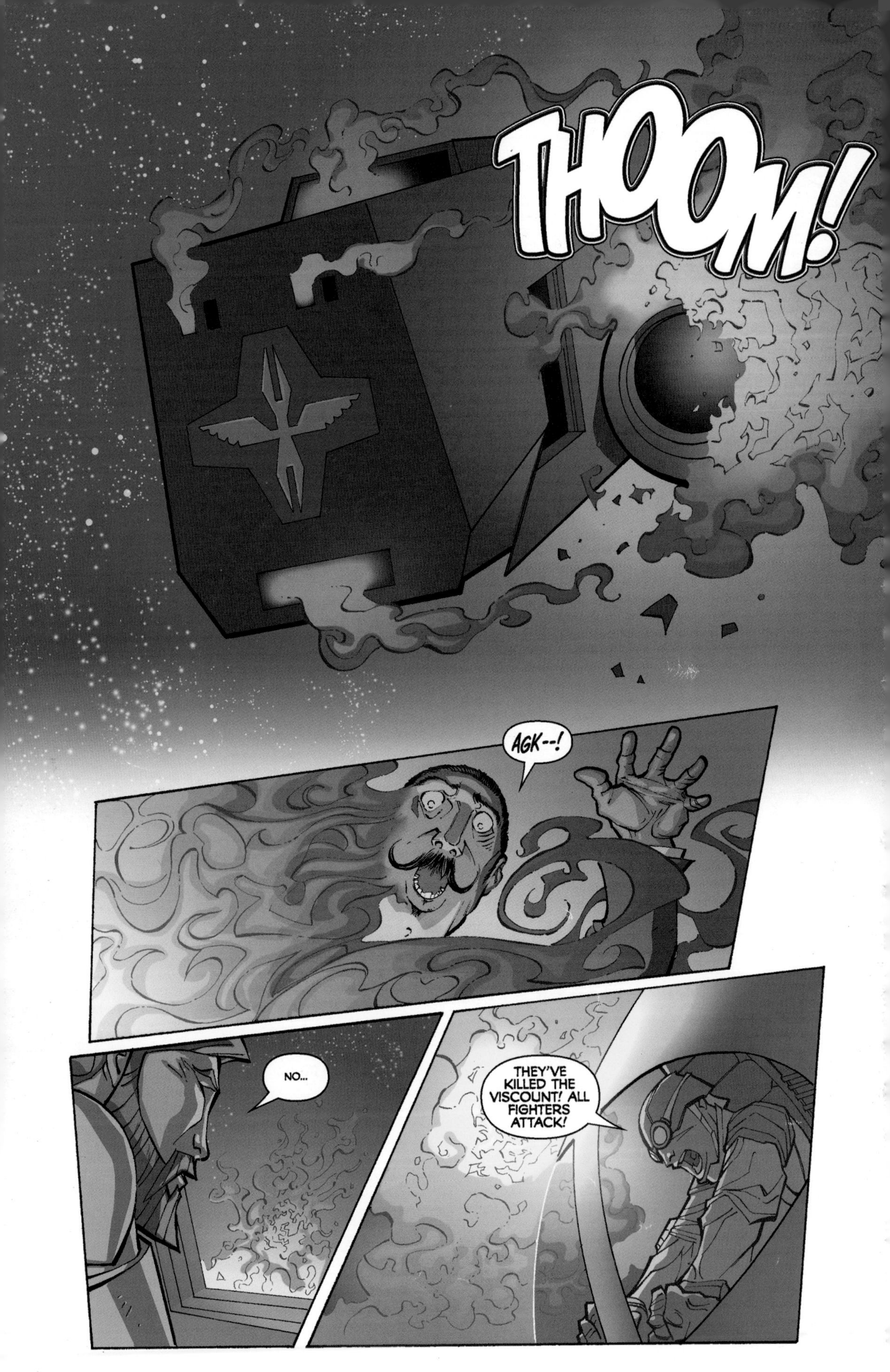
THOOM!
AGK--!
NO...
THEY'VE KILLED THE VISCOUNT! ALL FIGHTERS ATTACK!

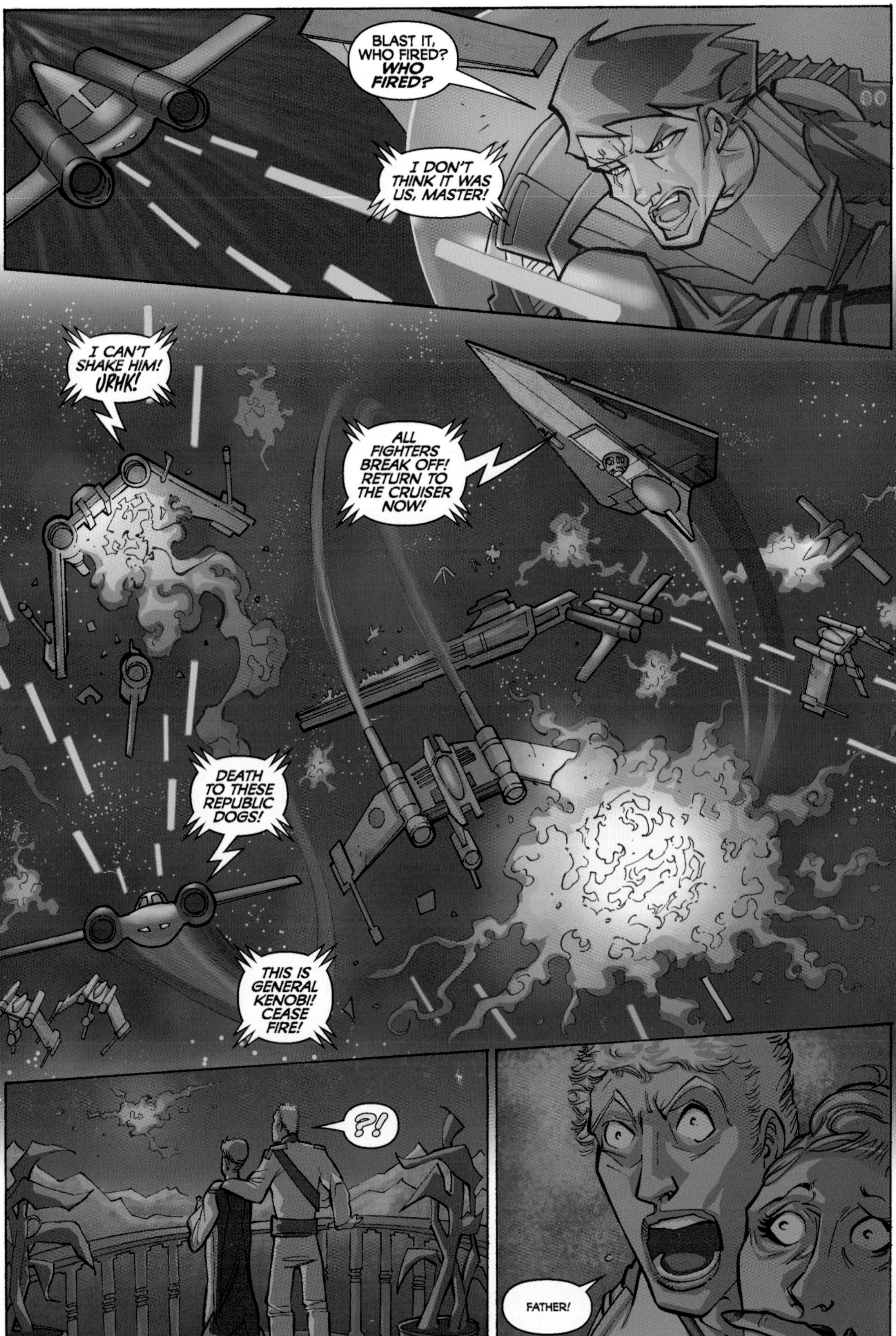
BLAST IT, WHO FIRED? WHO FIRED?
I DON'T THINK IT WAS US, MASTER!
I CAN'T SHAKE HIM! URHK!
ALL FIGHTERS BREAK OFF! RETURN TO THE CRUISER NOW!
DEATH TO THESE REPUBLIC DOGS!
THIS IS GENERAL KENOBI! CEASE FIRE!
?!
FATHER!

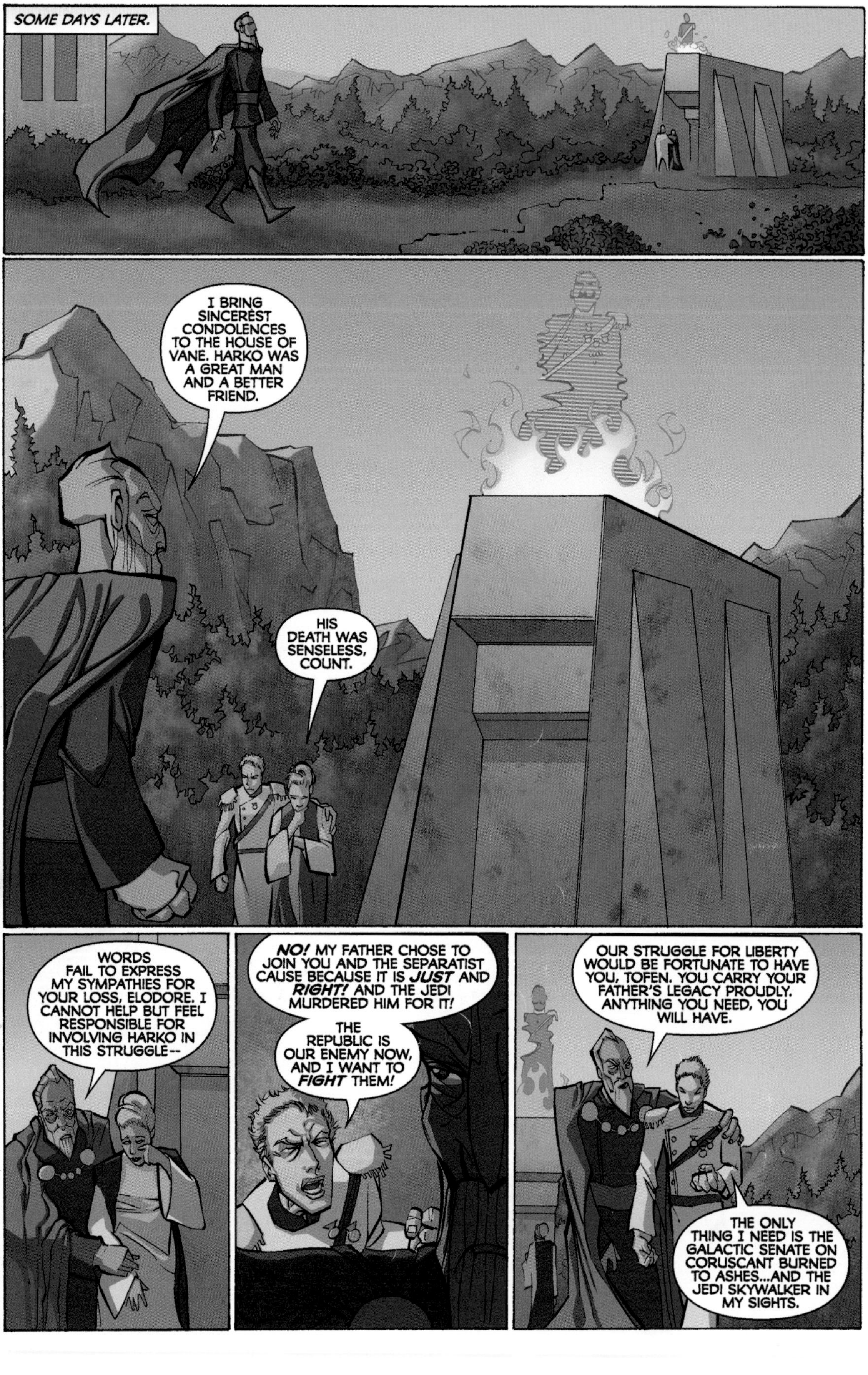
SOME DAYS LATER.
I BRING SINCEREST CONDOLENCES TO THE HOUSE OF VANE. HARKO WAS A GREAT MAN AND A BETTER FRIEND.
HIS DEATH WAS SENSELESS, COUNT.
WORDS FAIL TO EXPRESS MY SYMPATHIES FOR YOUR LOSS, ELODORE. I CANNOT HELP BUT FEEL RESPONSIBLE FOR INVOLVING HARKO IN THIS STRUGGLE--
NO! MY FATHER CHOSE TO JOIN YOU AND THE SEPARATIST CAUSE BECAUSE IT IS JUST AND RIGHT! AND THE JEDI MURDERED HIM FOR IT!
THE REPUBLIC IS OUR ENEMY NOW, AND I WANT TO FIGHT THEM!
OUR STRUGGLE FOR LIBERTY WOULD BE FORTUNATE TO HAVE YOU, TOFEN. YOU CARRY YOUR FATHER'S LEGACY PROUDLY. ANYTHING YOU NEED, YOU WILL HAVE.
THE ONLY THING I NEED IS THE GALACTIC SENATE ON CORUSCANT BURNED TO ASHES...AND THE JEDI SKYWALKER IN MY SIGHTS.

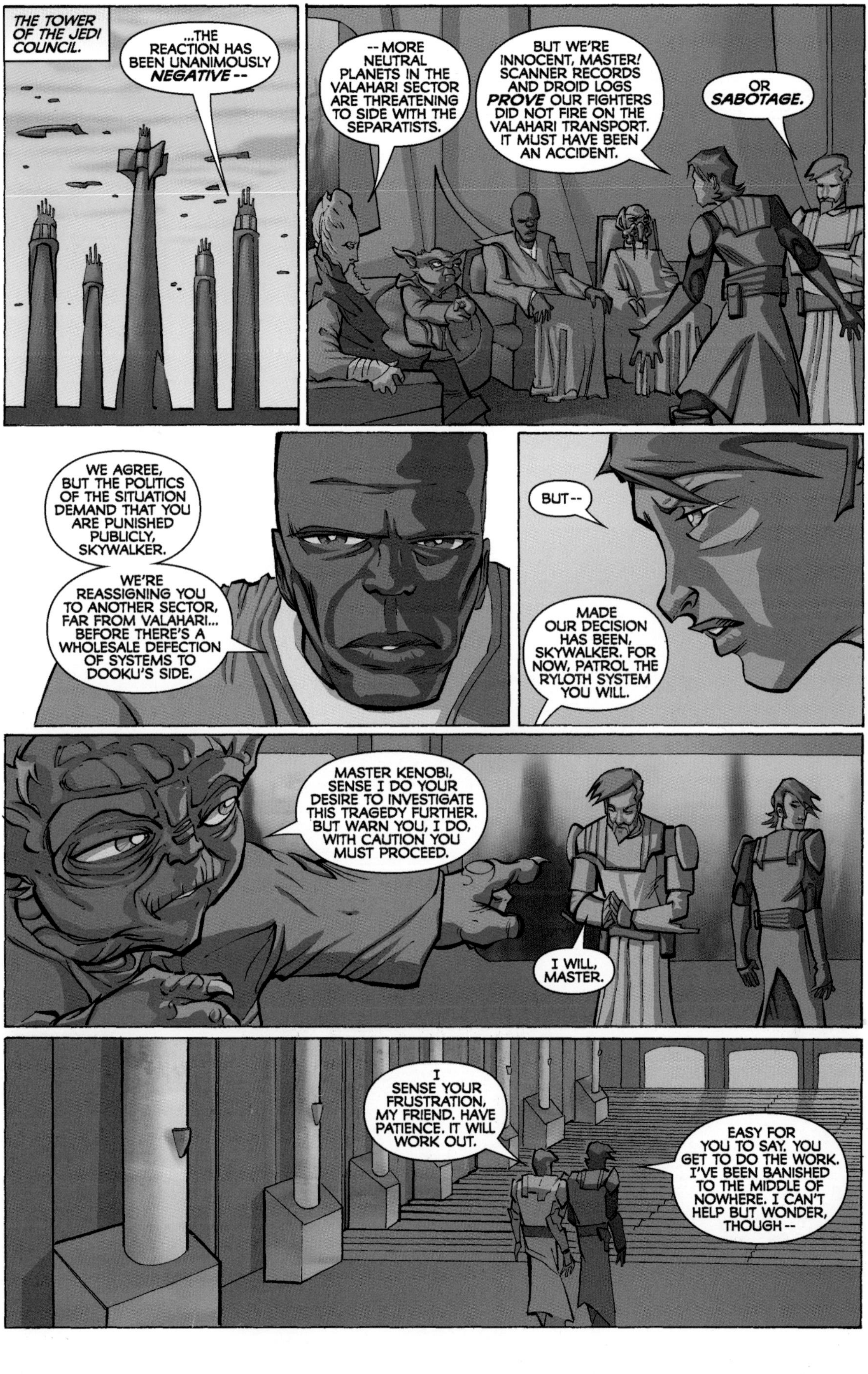
THE TOWER OF THE JEDI COUNCIL.
...THE REACTION HAS BEEN UNANIMOUSLY NEGATIVE --
-- MORE NEUTRAL PLANETS IN THE VALAHARI SECTOR ARE THREATENING TO SIDE WITH THE SEPARATISTS.
BUT WE'RE INNOCENT, MASTER! SCANNER RECORDS AND DROID LOGS PROVE OUR FIGHTERS DID NOT FIRE ON THE VALAHARI TRANSPORT. IT MUST HAVE BEEN AN ACCIDENT.
OR SABOTAGE.
WE AGREE, BUT THE POLITICS OF THE SITUATION DEMAND THAT YOU ARE PUNISHED PUBLICLY, SKYWALKER.
WE'RE REASSIGNING YOU TO ANOTHER SECTOR, FAR FROM VALAHARI... BEFORE THERE'S A WHOLESALE DEFECTION OF SYSTEMS TO DOOKU'S SIDE.
BUT --
MADE OUR DECISION HAS BEEN, SKYWALKER. FOR NOW, PATROL THE RYLOTH SYSTEM YOU WILL.
MASTER KENOBI, SENSE I DO YOUR DESIRE TO INVESTIGATE THIS TRAGEDY FURTHER. BUT WARN YOU, I DO, WITH CAUTION YOU MUST PROCEED.
I WILL, MASTER.
I SENSE YOUR FRUSTRATION, MY FRIEND. HAVE PATIENCE. IT WILL WORK OUT.
EASY FOR YOU TO SAY. YOU GET TO DO THE WORK. I'VE BEEN BANISHED TO THE MIDDLE OF NOWHERE. I CAN'T HELP BUT WONDER, THOUGH --

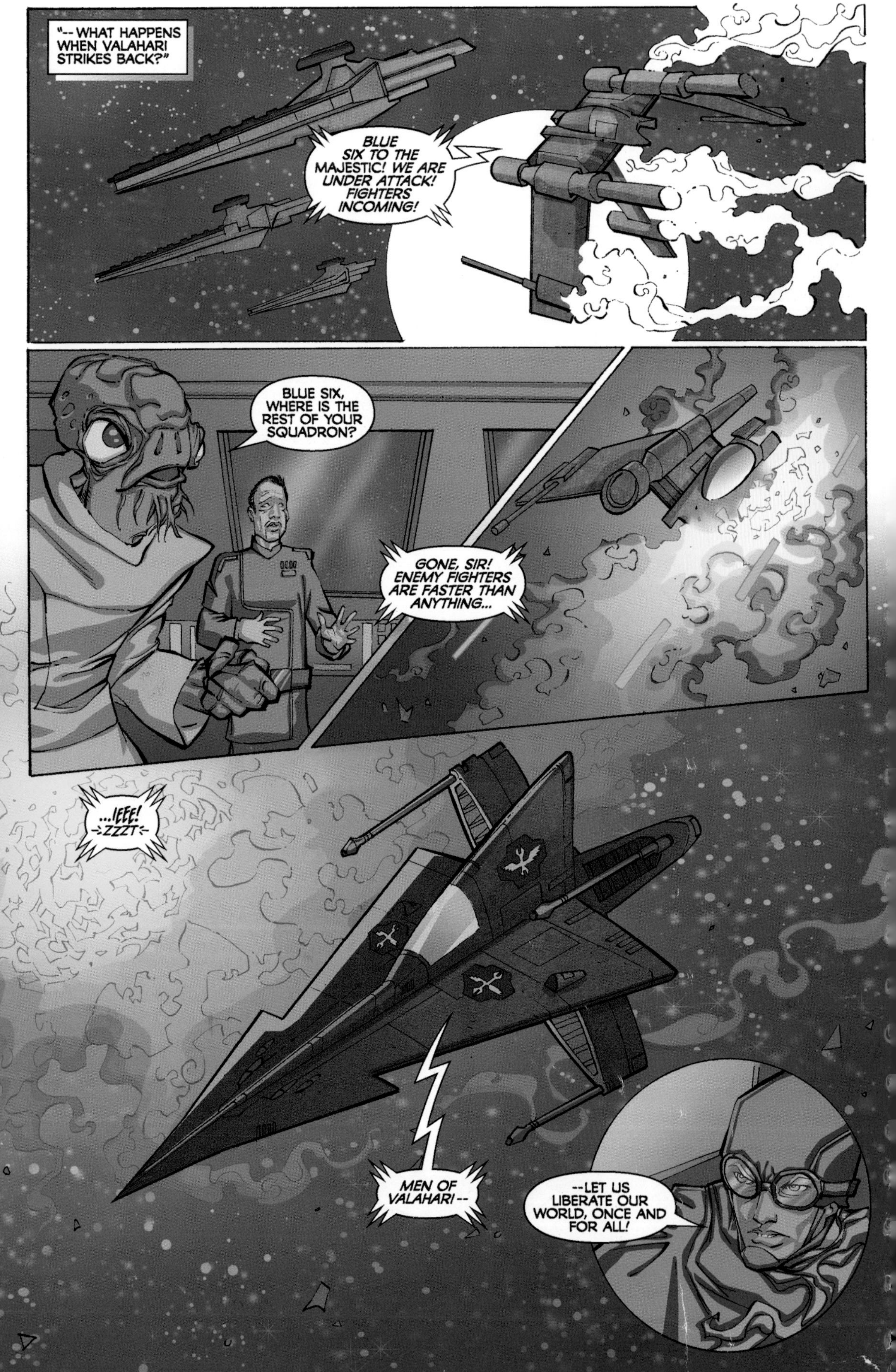
"-- WHAT HAPPENS WHEN VALAHARI STRIKES BACK?"
BLUE SIX TO THE MAJESTIC! WE ARE UNDER ATTACK! FIGHTERS INCOMING!
BLUE SIX, WHERE IS THE REST OF YOUR SQUADRON?
GONE, SIR! ENEMY FIGHTERS ARE FASTER THAN ANYTHING...
...IEEE! -ZZZT-
MEN OF VALAHARI --
--LET US LIBERATE OUR WORLD, ONCE AND FOR ALL!

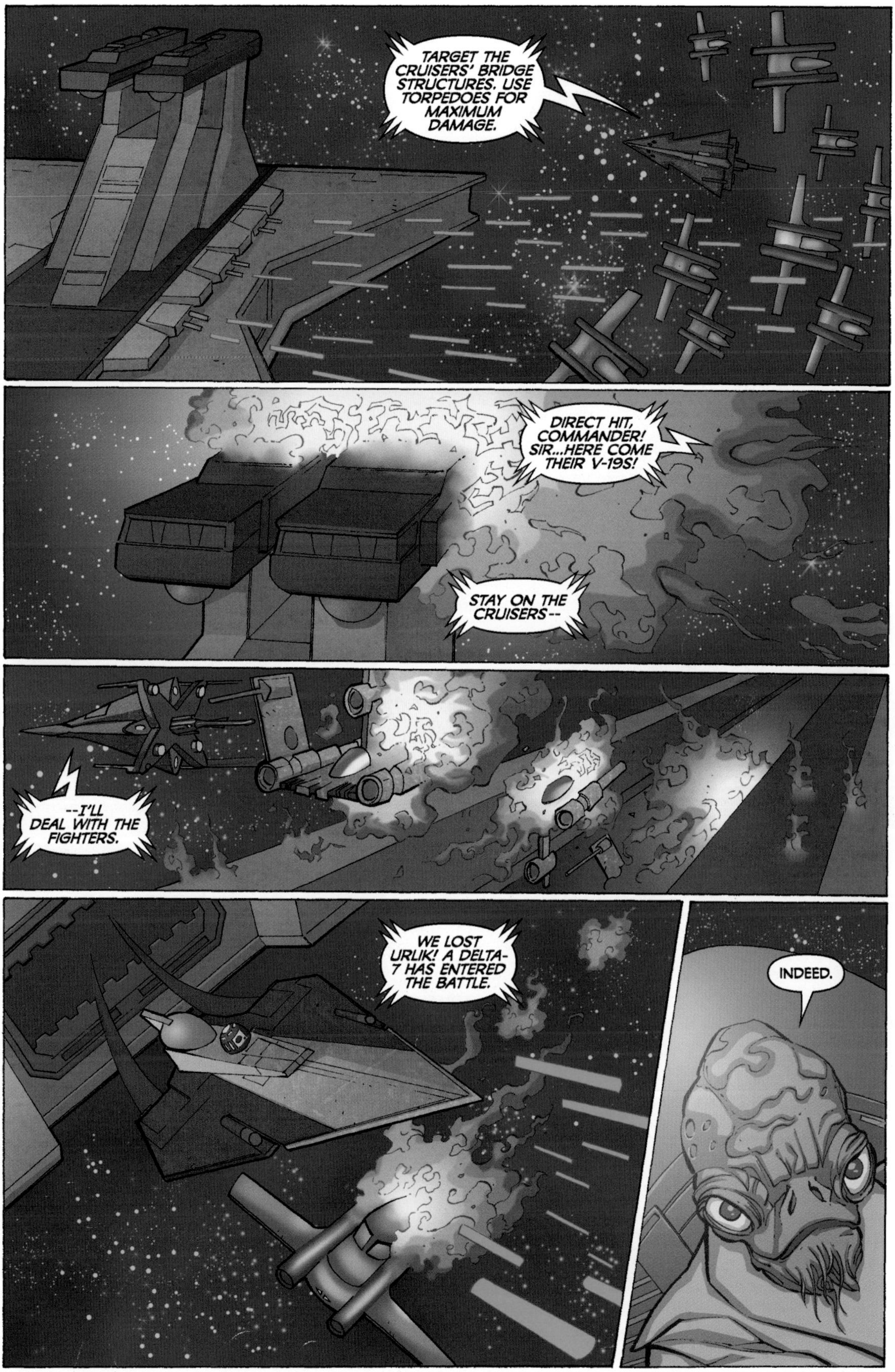
TARGET THE CRUISERS' BRIDGE STRUCTURES. USE TORPEDOES FOR MAXIMUM DAMAGE.
DIRECT HIT, COMMANDER! SIR...HERE COME THEIR V-19S!
STAY ON THE CRUISERS--
--I'LL DEAL WITH THE FIGHTERS.
WE LOST URLIK! A DELTA-7 HAS ENTERED THE BATTLE.
INDEED.

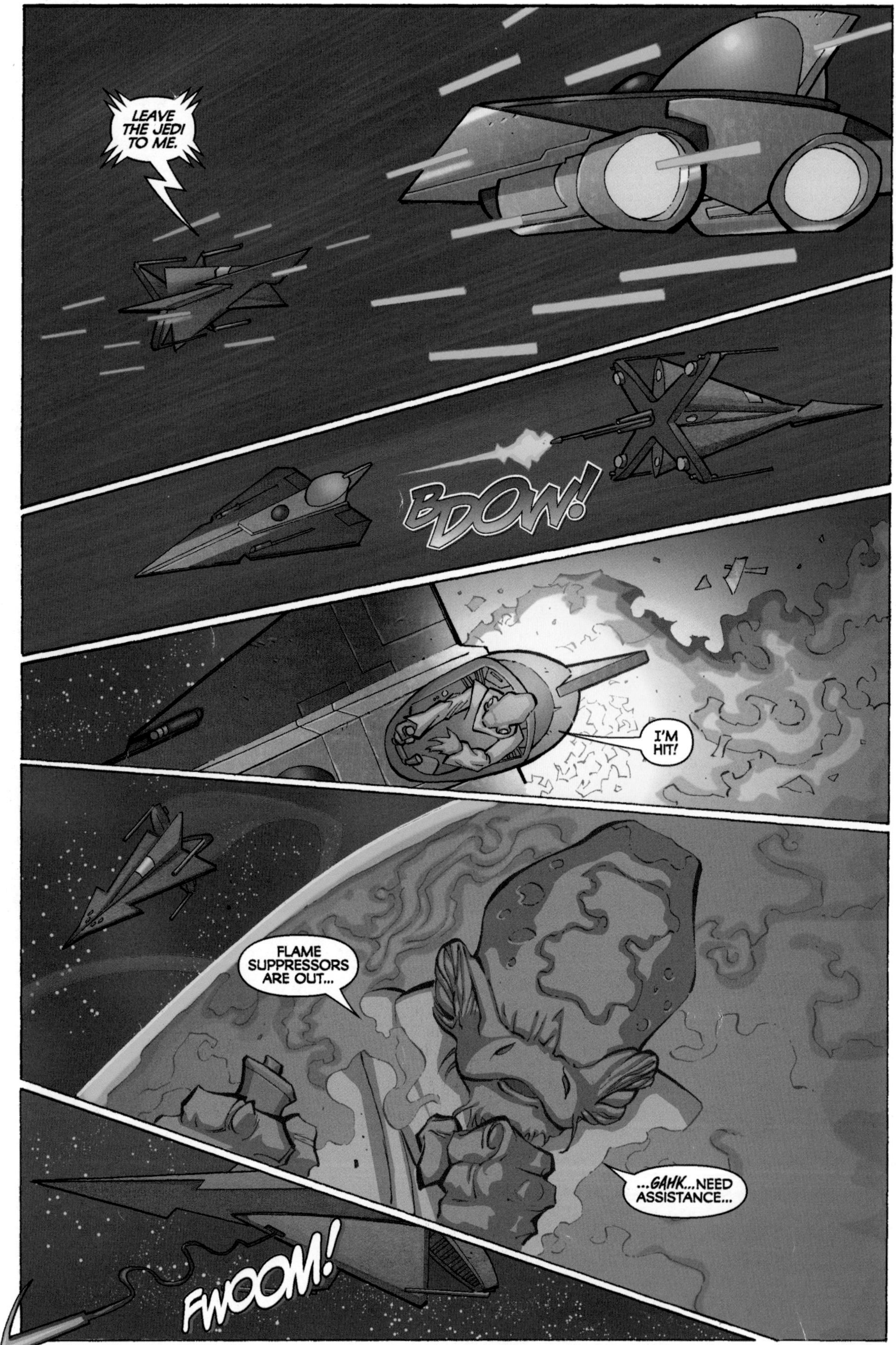
LEAVE THE JEDI TO ME.
BDOW!
I'M HIT!
FLAME SUPPRESSORS ARE OUT...
...GAHK...NEED ASSISTANCE...
FWOOM!

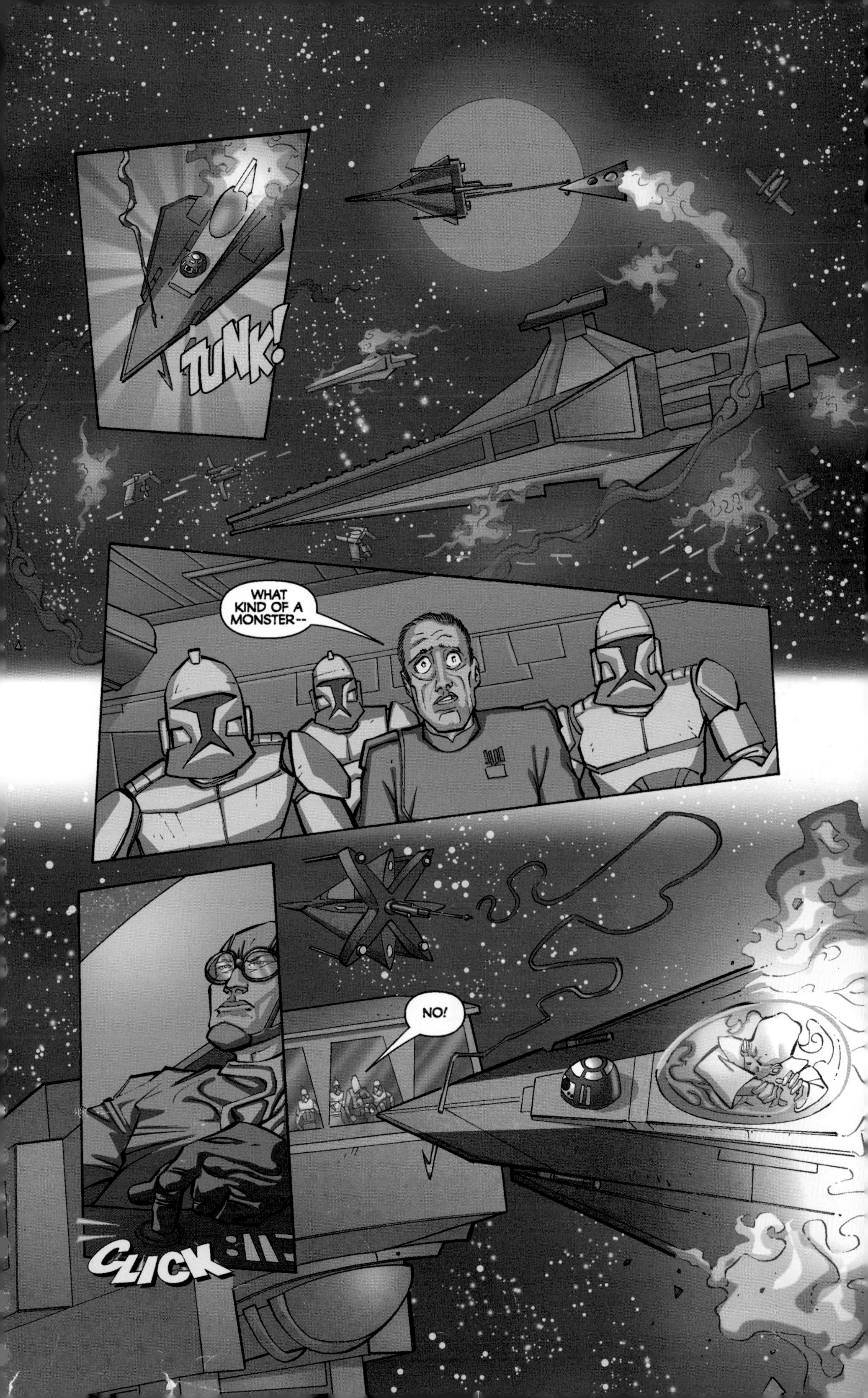
TUNK!
WHAT KIND OF A MONSTER--
NO!
CLICK

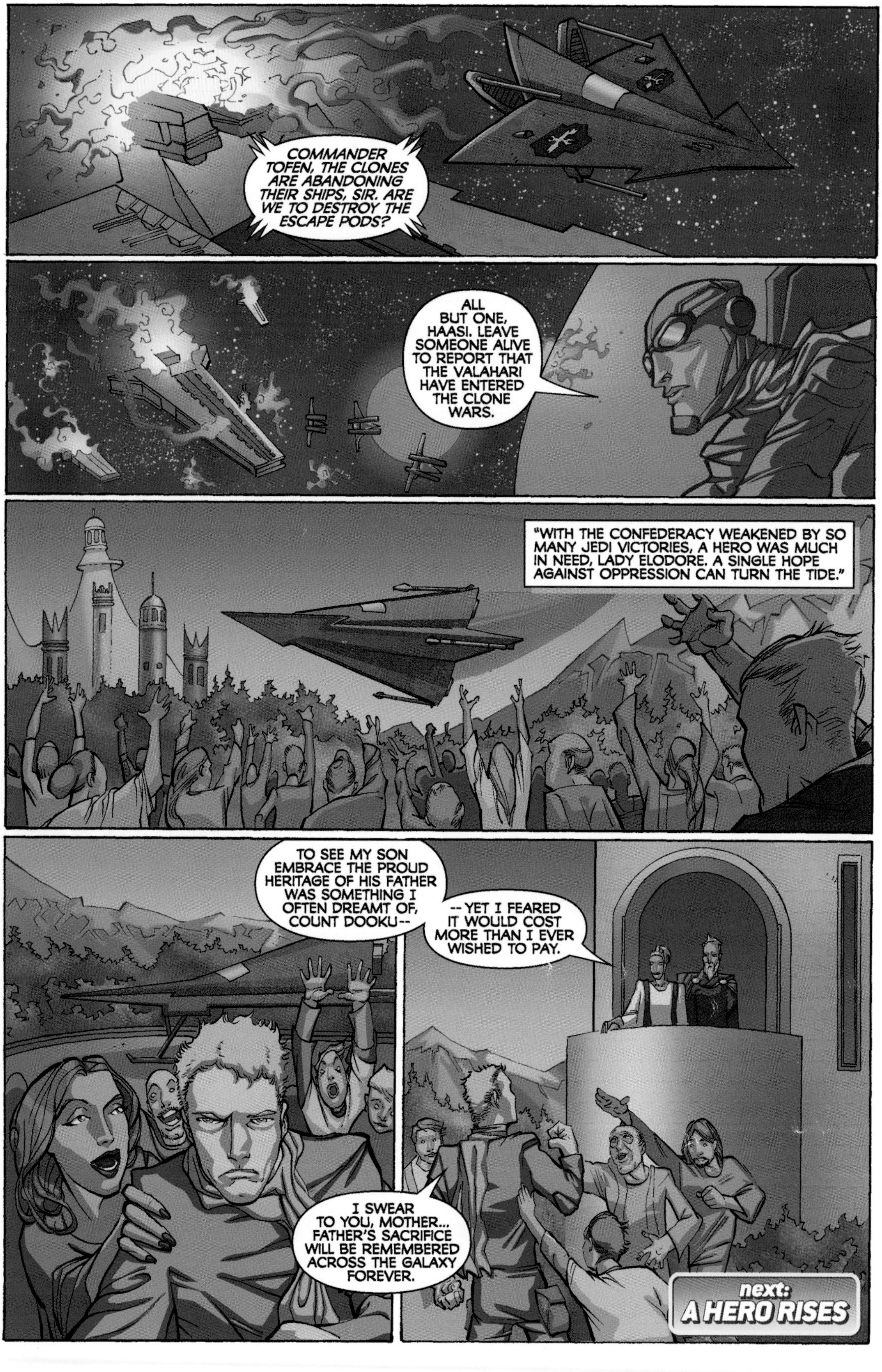
COMMANDER TOFEN, THE CLONES ARE ABANDONING THEIR SHIPS, SIR. ARE WE TO DESTROY THE ESCAPE PODS?
ALL BUT ONE, HAASI. LEAVE SOMEONE ALIVE TO REPORT THAT THE VALAHARI HAVE ENTERED THE CLONE WARS.
"WITH THE CONFEDERACY WEAKENED BY SO MANY JEDI VICTORIES, A HERO WAS MUCH IN NEED, LADY ELODORE. A SINGLE HOPE AGAINST OPPRESSION CAN TURN THE TIDE."
TO SEE MY SON EMBRACE THE PROUD HERITAGE OF HIS FATHER WAS SOMETHING I OFTEN DREAMT OF, COUNT DOOKU--
--YET I FEARED IT WOULD COST MORE THAN I EVER WISHED TO PAY.
I SWEAR TO YOU, MOTHER... FATHER'S SACRIFICE WILL BE REMEMBERED ACROSS THE GALAXY FOREVER.
next: A HERO RISES